# No Space

GW01066132

## Contents

# Chapter 1

## To Grow Potatoes...

When Jimmy Patterson asked his mother if he could grow potatoes, she said, "You can't grow potatoes here! You need lots of space."

That day at school, Jimmy asked his teacher, Mrs Bailey, about growing potatoes in the city.

"You need to have a big garden and a lot of fertilizer," she said. "How about taking care of our class plants during the holidays?"

When Jimmy got home,
he went to talk to his dad.
"I really want to grow potatoes,
but everyone says that I can't,"
Jimmy said sadly.

Jimmy's grandfather walked into the kitchen just at that moment.

"Well, now, Jimmy," he said. "I've got an idea."

"It won't take up too much space, will it, Grandad?"

"Used tyres don't take up much space, and they don't cost anything," said his grandfather.

"Tyres!" exclaimed Jimmy.

"Tyres," repeated his grandfather.

On the way home, Jimmy and his
grandfather stopped off at the garden
centre. Jimmy's grandfather asked for
one seed potato. The shop assistant
smiled when she saw the look on
Jimmy's face.

"One potato! Is that all?"
Jimmy exclaimed.

On the way home, Jimmy and his
grandfather stopped off at the garden
centre. Jimmy's grandfather asked for
one seed potato. The shop assistant
smiled when she saw the look on
Jimmy's face.

"One potato! Is that all?"
Jimmy exclaimed.

"We'd like a couple of old tyres,
and we may come back for a few
more in a month or two."

"No problem," said Bert.
"There are stacks of them out
the back. Help yourselves."

# Chapter 2

## Seed Potato

The next morning, Jimmy
and his grandfather walked
to the local garage.

"Hi, Bert! Could you do us a
favour?" asked Jimmy's grandfather.

"Sure thing," said Bert.

Jimmy's grandfather walked
into the kitchen just at that moment.

"Well, now, Jimmy," he said.
"I've got an idea."

"It won't take up too much space,
will it, Grandad?"

"Used tyres don't take up much
space, and they don't cost
anything," said his grandfather.

"Tyres!" exclaimed Jimmy.

"Tyres," repeated his grandfather.

Jimmy and his grandfather
rolled their tyres home.

"Now what?" asked Jimmy,
resting on his tyre in the garden.

"Yes, one potato is enough,"
said his grandfather.

"What are you going to do?"
the shop assistant asked.

"We're going to grow potatoes
in tyres," said Jimmy.

"What a great idea,"
said the shop assistant.

"Stack them on top of each other
in that sunny spot over there
and then we'll fill them with soil."
Jimmy's grandfather loosened
some soil with a spade.

"What next?" Jimmy asked
his grandfather eagerly.
"We add some water and
fertilizer," said his grandfather.

"Yes!" said his grandfather,
staring at the shoot. "It looks like
your potato's growing."

"Now what?" asked Jimmy.

"We just have to wait and watch,"
said his grandfather.

A week later, the potato shoot was growing fast. Jimmy and his grandfather regularly watered the plant and weeded around it. They gently turned the soil with a garden fork.

"Do you think we should give the potato plant some food, Grandad?" asked Jimmy.

"Hmmm... plant food... I wonder where we could find some?" said his grandfather.

Later that day, Mrs Curtis from next door came over.

"Your mother told me you're growing potatoes. I thought you could use some plant food."

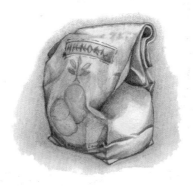

"Gee, thanks," said Jimmy.

"Don't forget to earth up!" she said.

"What's that?" asked Jimmy.

"You'll see after we go back to the garage for more tyres," said his grandfather.

# Chapter 4

## Earthing Up

By the weekend, there were four more old tyres lying beside the tyre mound. Jimmy and his grandfather carefully placed a third tyre on top.

"Now we have to put more soil
and some hay around the plant
as it grows. This keeps the potatoes
dark and warm. That's what
'earthing up' means," explained
Jimmy's grandfather.

At school the next day, Jimmy
asked Mrs Bailey if he could
have some of the hay they used
for the pet mice.

"Here you go, Jimmy," she said.

After school, Jimmy and his grandfather heaped the hay around the plant, tucking it under the rim of the tyre until only the potato leaves were poking through. Then they sprinkled water onto the hay.

The potato plant grew so fast that three more tyres were needed. Now six tyres were stacked in the corner outside.

Just over three weeks later,
while Jimmy was doing his daily
potato check, he yelled out, "Come
quick, Grandad. It's got flowers!"

"Great!" said his grandfather,
looking at the plant.

After several weeks, the flowers died off and the leaves slowly turned yellow.

"Why has the potato plant died?" asked Jimmy.

"Because it's time to harvest our crop," said his grandfather.

## Chapter 5

## Harvest Time!

Everyone came out to watch.

"Now," said Jimmy's grandfather, "we take off one tyre at a time."

At first, all that happened was that a mass of soil and hay fell to the ground.

"We'll clean that up later," said
Jimmy's grandfather, as they carefully
lifted the next tyre up and over
the yellow leaves of the plant. More
soil and hay fell to the ground.

"No potatoes," said Jimmy,
in a disappointed voice.

"Patience," said his grandfather, prodding the soil with his foot. "Here we go!"

One baby potato and two larger potatoes lay half-hidden in the soil.

"Next tyre, please!"

They pulled off the third tyre. Four large potatoes rolled out.

"Hey, look!" yelled Jimmy.

"Keep going, Jimmy," said his grandfather.

The fourth tyre came off. Twenty large potatoes sat in the soil.
The next tyre revealed some more potatoes, smaller and bumpier than the others, but still good. The last tyre had three little potatoes.

"All that from *one* potato!" said Jimmy. "Now who said you can't grow potatoes in the city?"

"*We did*!" cried everyone.
"But we were wrong!"

 # From the Author

 My grandfather taught me about growing things in buckets, and my three children loved growing potatoes in tyres. Buckets, pots, and tyres can make good gardens for people who have no growing space outdoors. Try it some time!

Beatrice Hale

 # From the Illustrator

 I live in Christchurch, New Zealand, with my husband and two sons. My husband is an agronomist, so he helped me with the resources to illustrate *No Space to Waste*. I think that growing potatoes in a tyre stack looks like fun. I'd like to give it a try.

Annabel Craighead